FIRST FIRE

A TRADITIONAL NATIVE AMERICAN TALE

MariJo Moore

Illustrated by Anthony Chee Emerson

Rigby

A long, very long time ago, the world
was cold because there was no fire.
So the Thunderers sent lightning and
put fire in the bottom of a hollow tree
that grew on a little green island.

The animals across the blue waters knew fire was on the island. They could see smoke rising from the tree. They wanted the fire to keep them warm. But how could they get it? They held a big meeting to talk about their problem.

Every animal that could fly or swim wanted
to be the one to bring back the fire.

"I'm the obvious choice," boasted Raven.
"I'm the best thinker."

The other animals agreed, so off he went.
Flying high and far across the waters, Raven
landed on top of the tree with the fire.
He looked down and saw its burning
orange glow.

"Hmm," he thought. "How will I get it
back across the water? It seems very hot.
I'm sure an idea will come to me soon."

But as Raven sat
thinking, he didn't notice
that the heat from the fire
was scorching his feathers.
He started to grow
hotter and hotter,
until . . .

"SQUAWK!" He quickly flew away and
plunged into the water to cool down,
but his feathers stayed black forever.

Back at the meeting, Little
Screech Owl was flapping up and
down. "Let me try! Oh please!" she
asked. "I won't be as foolish as Raven."

So Little Screech Owl flew off to
the island.

"Fire is so pretty," Little Screech Owl thought, "but so hot! How will I get it back across the water?"

She put her head inside the tree. Suddenly . . .

"SCREECH!" A blast of hot air came up and almost burned her eyes. She quickly flew away and plunged into the water to cool down, but her eyes stayed red forever.

Back at the meeting, Hooting Owl and
Horned Owl were getting fed up.

"If you want a job done right," they
hooted, "you have to do it yourself."
And off they flew to the little island,
laughing at poor Raven and Little Screech
Owl as they passed them in the water.

By the time they got to the hollow tree, the fire was burning very fiercely.

"OK, let's just get a little closer," said Hooting Owl.

Both owls peered over the edge of the hollow tree, and . . .

"SQUAWK!" The smoke almost blinded them. The ashes carried up by the winds made white rings around their eyes. They quickly flew away and plunged into the water to cool down, but the white rings never went away.

Having seen their friends get burned,
no other birds would even dare to try to
get the fire. The animals looked around
for someone else to go.

"Excuse me," said a small voice. The
animals looked down to see Little
Racing Snake.

"I think I have an idea," she said.

No one else had any better ideas,
so they agreed to let her try.

Little Racing Snake swam through the blue waters to the island and crawled through the grass.

"The only way to do this is headfirst!" she declared, and she wriggled into the tree through a small hole at the bottom. But suddenly . .

"HISS!" The heat and the smoke were too much for Little Racing Snake. Her body was burned black as she darted over the hot ashes. She finally plunged into the water to cool down, but to this day she darts about as if she is still trying to get over the hot ashes.

Back at the meeting, Great Blacksnake
was shaking his head and tutting loudly.

"I'll be able to get the fire," he declared.
"After all, I'm the best at climbing."

Great Blacksnake slithered into the water
and swam over to the island.

When he got there, Great Blacksnake started climbing the tree.

"This will be as easy as pie!" he laughed, as he got closer to the top. But instead of stopping and thinking at the top, he dived right into the burning tree. Well, you can guess what happened next!

"HISS!" Poor Great Blacksnake yelped and screamed and jumped up out of the fire as fast as lightning! He plunged into the water to cool down, but not before he was burned black forever.

Back on the island the animals were complaining.

"I'm cold," shivered Bullfrog.

"I'm freezing!" agreed Chipmunk. "But who will go get the fire?"

Suddenly, all the animals found other things to do. They didn't want to be the ones to go. They were in no hurry to burn themselves into a new look, no matter how cold their world might be.

"I'll go," said a little voice from above.
The animals looked up and saw Water
Spider swinging from a thread above
their heads.

"All the time you have been getting
burned or making excuses for not going,
I have been thinking hard about the best
solution. And I think I know what it is."

The animals all felt a bit embarrassed that a little spider had been a better thinker than they were, but icicles were starting to form on the ends of their noses, so they agreed to let Water Spider go.

The little spider spun a tiny bowl and placed it on her strong back. She swam across the blue waters to the green island and scurried through the grass to the tree.

Water Spider climbed in through a
hole in the bottom of the tree and very
carefully took one little burning coal. She
put this into the small bowl on her back,
then she swam back across the top of
the blue waters.

That night Bullfrog and Chipmunk put
sticks on the tiny burning coal. It grew
and grew into a huge, glowing fire that
seemed to light up the world.

Some of the animals decided to celebrate and invited Water Spider as their guest of honor. But Water Spider invited the birds and snakes to join her, because they had also tried to bring the fire. She believed that the only way to fail was not to try in the first place.

So, the birds, snakes, and four-legged animals gathered around the huge, glowing fire that night, happily sharing stories in the warmth.

All of this happened a long, very long time ago.